Space and Time Magic

Mark Jeffrey Stefik

Illustrated by Mark & Barbara Stefik

The Oberlanders: Book 9

Space and Time Magic

The Oberlanders

Published by Portola Publishing
Portola Valley, Ca. 94028 USA

© 2021 by Mark Jeffrey Stefik

Illustrations for the book are by Mark Jeffrey Stefik and Barbara Stefik.

This book is a work of fiction. The characters, incidents, and dialogue are drawn from the author's imagination and are not to be construed as real. Any resemblance to actual events or persons, living or dead, is entirely coincidental.

Space and Time Magic the ninth book in *The Oberlanders*. The books describe fictional events in a universe including the planets Sol #3 and Zorcon.

Further information about the series can be found at
www.PortolaPublishing.com

Library of Congress Cataloging-in-Publication Data
Copyright Office Registration Number:
Stefik, Mark Jeffrey
    Space and Time Magic / Mark Jeffrey Stefik
Edition 3
ISBN: 978-1-943176-19-9

Space and Time Magic

The Zorconians had tapped into the core of their sun to harvest energy for everything they did. Now their sun was ready to explode. Zorcon's desperate High Council decided to send an armed fleet to establish a settlement on Sol #3. Meanwhile in Oberland Kingdom, a crone appeared in Cinderwan's mirror. Cinderwan remembered facing Baba Yaga in the woods as a small child. In the greatest test of her life, she would revisit her childhood experiences. She would need all of her training to meet a challenge in the metaverse. And the help of her friends.

Space and Time Magic

Books in *The Oberlanders*

Magic with Side Effects (#1)

Magic Misspoken (#2)

Old Magic Awakens (#3)

Magic Reprogrammed (#4)

Earth Magic (#5)

Fire Magic (#6)

Water Magic (#7)

Air Magic (#8)

Space and Time Magic (#9)

The Sendroids series continues after *The Oberlanders*. Information about both series can be found on the website www.PortolaPublishing.com

Space and Time Magic

ACKNOWLEDGMENTS

Thank you to our wonderful friends and early readers who read earlier versions of the folktales of *The Oberlanders* as we developed them. Special thanks to Asli Aydin, Phil Berghausen, Eric and Emma Bier, Danny Bobrow, J.J. and Stu Card, Nilesh and Laura Doctor, Ollie Eggiman, Lance Good, Craig Heberer, Chris Kavert, Ray and Lois Kuntz, Raj and Zoe Minhas, Ranjeeta Prakash, Mary Ann Puppo, Jamie Richard, Lynne Russell, Mali Sarpangal, Jackie Shek, Morgan Stefik, Sebastian Steiger, Frank Torres, Paige Turner, Blanca Vargas, Barry and Joyce Vissell, Alan and Pam Wu, Meili Xu, and their kids and young relatives.

Thank you also to the people of Gimmelwald and Mürren, Switzerland in the Swiss Alps and the people of Vetan in Valle d'Aosta in the Italian Alps. These places inspired us with their natural beauty and stillness, and the power of the mountains, lakes, forests, and waterfalls. The people of the Alps have histories and traditions that reach back into legend and folktale.

Space and Time Magic

CONTENTS

Space and Time Magic

"Before she could fulfill her destiny, Cinderwan first had to remember and understand her childhood." Prof. Andreacus Steficus, Department of Cosmology, Zorcon University. *Cosmic Midwifery: Genesis and Causality in the Multiverse.*

Space and Time Magic

1 Cinderwan's Dream

 inderwan sat by the fireplace in her lakeside home, waiting for Jorgan. The asteroid crisis was past. They had spent the day helping villagers returning from the emergency camp in Hidden Valley.

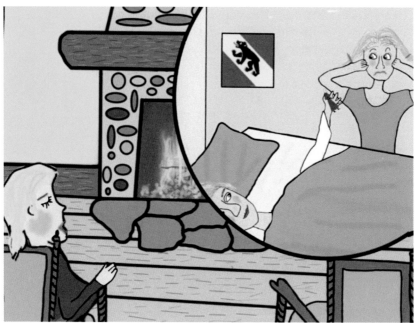

"Here is a doll for you, Vasalisa."

Cinderwan was sleepy. As she rested her eyes, she heard Baba Yaga whisper, "Once upon a time there was, and once upon a time there was not."

She settled in and began to dream. She heard the voice of Bodi, her mother. Bodi said, "Vasalisa, my dear. Listen carefully."

Cinderella saw her younger self as a little girl sitting by a bed. It was her mother's death bed.

She had not heard the name "Vasalisa" for a long time. Vasalisa was her childhood name. Everyone had called her Vasalisa before her stepmother arrived.

It was difficult for little Vasalisa to listen to her mother. "My dear daughter, challenges will come to you. Do not face them with resentment or bitterness. The challenges will prepare you for your future, but they are not the meaning of your life."

Bodi took a tiny doll from beneath the covers of her bed. She whispered to Vasalisa, "I am near to my last breath, my daughter. This doll is for you. She will appear when you need her. Let her be your secret. If you need help, you can ask the doll. Feed her when you take your meals. She is my blessing for you."

Then Bodi closed her eyes. She took her last breath and was still.

Cinderwan recognized the dream. It was a memory from her childhood.

After her mother died, Vasalisa and her father grieved for a long time. He was often away from home working to support them. After some years, her father met a widow with two daughters. He married the widow and Vasalisa got a stepmother. Her stepmother and stepsisters smiled and appeared to be nice, but they were secretly cruel to Vasalisa. When Vasalisa's father was away, they made her their servant.

Vasalisa was kind and became more beautiful and sweeter as she grew up. The stepsisters resented and hated Vasalisa. They grew twisted and mean over time.

One day a man came to the castle to tell them that Vasalisa's father had become ill and died. Vasalisa's stepmother was grim. She told Cinderella that she would need to stop going to Oberland School. Instead, she would do work around the castle. They would have little food to eat. Vasalisa would need to clean, cook the food, tend the fire, and run errands. Vasalisa worked hard. She did not complain.

2 The Stepsisters' Trick

ife was not easy for Vasalisa. Her stepmother told her to eat only leftover food scraps. Her stepsisters ordered her to do more and more chores. "Wash the floor! Find my dress. Fix this ribbon. Mind the stove. Fetch some water. Clean the dishes. Comb my hair!" Their hatred withered their hearts. The stepsisters were never satisfied or happy.

"From now on we'll call you Cinderella."

Vasalisa chopped wood and tended the fire. It was hard to keep the ashes from her clothing. Her stepsisters teased her. "You are always dusty with cinders. We will call you Cinderella!" They found it amusing to deprive Vasalisa of her given name. The stepsisters clapped their hands with joy.

One day, the stepsisters conspired to get rid of Cinderella. Although they never tended a fire, they knew how to put one out. "We will tell Mother that Cinderella let the fire go out. She will send her into the forest to Baba Yaga to get fire. Baba Yaga will kill her and eat her." The stepsisters giggled at their evil plan and waited for Cinderella to come home from her errands.

Baba Yaga lived in a hut with chicken legs.

Baba Yaga was an old crone with crooked teeth. She flew in a wooden bucket that she rowed with her broom. She may not have been wicked, but she suffered no fools. She lived deep in the forest in a house with chicken legs. The house could walk around, whirl and even dance.

The castle was dark when Cinderella came back after her errands. Her stepmother said, "You are a stupid child! You let the fire go out. We cannot cook. We have no light. Someone will have to fetch fire for us. I am too tired. Your stepsisters are too afraid. You must get fire for us."

In the background Cinderella saw her stepsisters pretending to be afraid. They winked and smiled at each other, pleased that their trick was working.

Cinderella felt her anger rise. Although she was small, she felt very strong. She could push her stepmother aside and go after her stepsisters. They had tormented her long enough. Now was the time to set things right.

"You must get fire for us."

Before Cinderella could act on this thought, she felt the doll jumping in her pocket. The doll said, "Do not seek revenge, Vasalisa. Your future is bigger than your stepfamily. Go into the forest and find Baba Yaga. Do this for your own reasons and for your own destiny."

As the doll spoke, Vasalisa felt her anger fade away. She smiled at her stepfamily and said, "Yes. I will do that."

3 Into the Dark Forest

t was dark in the forest. Vasalisa put her hand into her pocket and found her doll. She felt a little better. As the paths twisted and forked in the woods, she asked her doll, "Which way should I go?" Each time the doll answered, "go to the right" or "go to the left" or "go straight ahead."

"Is this Baba Yaga's hut?"

Vasalisa shivered. She felt a cold chill running up her back. Ahead was a hut in the woods. It was a strange place, surrounded by a fence made of skulls and bones. The hut stood on two chicken legs. Eerie light glowed out of its windows.

"Is this Baba Yaga's hut?" Vasalisa asked her doll.

Vasalisa felt the doll in her pocket shaking. It was laughing.

"Let's see," said the doll. "The hut is in the dark forest. Check. It is surrounded by skulls on bones and sticks. Check. The hut has chicken legs. Check. Things are spooky and scary around here. Check."

Vasalisa laughed despite her fears. She wasn't expecting humor from the doll, but now she felt better. "OK, I get it," she said.

"You *already know* the answer," continued the doll. "It may be frightening, but this *is* the hut of Baba Yaga."

"Vasalisa felt a breeze as something swooped down from the tops of the trees. It was the fearsome crone. Baba Yaga did not ride in a carriage or on a horse. She flew in a bucket. She rowed the bucket with her broom and steered it with a mop. Her hair streamed behind her. She smelled.

Baba Yaga flew in a wooden bucket.

Baba Yaga faced the young Vasalisa, "What is it you want, child? Don't just stand there looking at me. Why are you here? Is there something that you want?" She did not wait for answers. She just pummeled Vasalisa with questions.

"I am here to ask for fire," Vasalisa answered. "Our family fire has gone out. We have no heat and no light."

"Why should I help you?" asked Baba Yaga. "Why should I give you anything? Perhaps I will just eat you for my dinner!"

Vasalisa felt the doll jumping in her pocket. The doll was thinking. "Baba Yaga can be difficult. She does not like long answers. Just say 'Because I ask.'"

Vasalisa looked directly at the crone. "Because I ask," she said.

The crone frowned. "Luck is with you," she replied. "That is a good answer."

4 Three Tasks for Vasalisa

aba Yaga continued, "I cannot just give you things. First, you must prove yourself worthy. If you succeed at doing my three tasks, I will give you fire. If not, my child, you will be my dinner!" The old crone cackled.

"Tonight, you must separate the corn into two piles."

Baba Yaga looked at Vasalisa and added, "Also, don't speak unless you are spoken to. And don't ask too many questions. With luck, you may learn something."

Vasalisa wanted to ask her, "How many questions are too many?" but the doll jumped in her pocket.

"Say nothing," whispered the doll.

Baba Yaga looked closely at Vasalisa again, as if she expected her to say something. When Vasalisa remained silent, Baba Yaga hopped out of her bucket and ran to the front door of her hut. "Follow me," she said.

Inside, the hut was messy and dirty. Mice played on the floor. There were spiders and webs. Black crows sat wherever they pleased.

Baba Yaga ordered Vasalisa to bring her dinner. In the oven Vasalisa found a feast of food, enough to feed ten people. Baba Yaga ate it all and then burped a great burp. When she was finished, all that was left was a crust of bread and a little soup. She gave that to Vasalisa.

"Now, child, wash my clothes. Sweep my yard. Straighten this place up! It is dirty and it is a mess!" Baba Yaga paused for a moment, rolling her evil eyes. Then she pointed to a pile on a table and continued, "On this table is a pile of corn. Tonight, you must separate the corn into two piles. One pile should contain only the spoiled and mildewed corn. The other pile should have the good and fresh corn. Do it carefully. I will check your work."

With that, Baba Yaga rolled over on her bed and fell asleep. The room filled with the sound of her snoring. Vasalisa shuddered. Her time with Baba Yaga was even worse than her life with her stepmother and stepsisters.

Vasalisa whispered quietly to her doll as Baba Yaga snored. "What should I do? I can never complete these tasks by morning."

The doll whispered back to her, "Do not worry, Vasalisa. Eat and sleep. I will take care of everything."

Vasalisa took a little of the crust of bread and soup and put it in her pocket. The doll ate it. Then Vasalisa ate some bread herself and went to a corner of the hut. She fell asleep.

In the morning, sunlight came into the hut. Vasalisa got up. The crone had left during the night. All of the work was done except that Baba Yaga's dinner still needed to be cooked.

In the evening, there was a thump as Baba Yaga landed in her bucket. Baba Yaga kicked open the front door. She narrowed her eyes and looked around the room looking for something wrong. When she found nothing, she turned to Vasalisa. "This time you are lucky!" she said.

Baba Yaga called on her servants to grind the corn. Two hands appeared in the air and began to crush the good corn. Bits of corn flew in the air. The hands took the bad corn and cooked it on the stove, making an odorous brew. Finally, Baba Yaga sat down to eat. She ate the corn mush, drank the brew, and burped.

Baba Yaga then pointed out the door to a great mound of soil on a table in the yard. She turned to Vasalisa and said, "There is a pile of dirt with thousands of sesame seeds in it. In the morning, I want to have the sesame seeds separated neatly from the soil. Do this properly, or it will not go well for you!"

Again, Baba Yaga laid down to sleep and snored loudly. Vasalisa watched her sleep and whispered to her doll, "How can I possibly do this?"

She went into the yard and started to pick out the sesame seeds. Vasalisa saw evil crows in the yard, watching her work.

"The crone plans to trick you. After you sort the sesame seeds, the crows will eat them," whispered the doll. "Bring me a glass jar and then go to sleep. All will be well."

Vasalisa saw evil crows in the yard, watching her work.

Vasalisa found a jar. She cleaned it and brought it to the doll. Then she gave the doll part of her meager dinner and ate some herself. Afterwards Vasalisa fell asleep in the yard.

When she woke in the morning the sesame seeds were nicely stored in the clean jar. Baba Yaga and the crows were gone. Vasalisa started to prepare dinner for Baba Yaga.

Evening came. There was a thump as Baba Yaga landed in the yard in her bucket. She looked at the pile of dirt on the ground and the sparkling jar of sesame seeds. "Lucky for you that you were able to do this for me," she said. She said nothing about the jar or her crows. Again, Baba Yaga called for her servant hands. The hands appeared in the air. They pressed the sesame seeds into a greasy oil.

Baba Yaga drank the sesame oil as it was, smacked her lips, and burped. Then she ate the stew that Vasalisa had prepared. She smiled but said nothing.

"Tomorrow I have one more task for you, child. Perform it well and I will give you fire. But if you are unworthy or fail at the task, it will not go well for you."

"We will have three jars for the beans."

Vasalisa shuddered. Baba Yaga's tasks were getting more difficult. They required skillful choices. What would be next?

"There are thousands of beans on the table in the yard," said Baba Yaga. "Some of the beans are sprouting. I don't eat the sprouted and unsprouted beans at the same time. Before the sun rises, separate the sprouted beans from the unsprouted ones." With that the old crone cackled. She turned in her bed and went to sleep.

Vasalisa sensed that the crone was feigning sleep and listening. She walked outside and hopped down to the ground. When she was out of hearing range of the crone, she fed the doll and herself.

Vasalisa whispered quietly to her doll, "This is another trick. The beans will keep sprouting. If I separate the sprouted beans now, more beans will sprout during the night. But if I wait until morning, there won't be enough time to separate them."

"I'll have you now, my pretty!"

The doll nodded. "This task sounds difficult. What will you do?"

Vasalisa thought out loud. "We could water the beans. They might all sprout by morning. We would have no work to do!"

The doll was quiet. Then she asked, "That may be wishful thinking. If any of the beans remain unsprouted, what will Baba Yaga do?"

"I see," said Vasalisa. "Well, here is another idea. We prepare three jars for the beans. The first jar is for beans that are dried up. The last jar is for the beans that have already sprouted. The middle jar is for beans that have not sprouted yet, but which may sprout by morning."

"What a clever idea!" said the doll. "We can do most of the sorting now. When morning comes, we will only have to check the middle jar of mixed sprouted and unsprouted beans. Then you can move the few remaining beans that sprouted during the night."

Before sunrise, Vasalisa was awakened by a cackle of glee. "I'll have you now, my pretty," exclaimed Baba Yaga.

The crone was dancing wildly.

Vasalisa opened her eyes. Baba Yaga was not watching Vasalisa. She was dancing wildly around the yard. The crone rubbed her hands and smiled.

The doll whispered to Vasalisa. "Say nothing. Bow your head. Take the sprouted beans from the mixed bean jar and move them to the sprouted bean jar."

Vasalisa quickly moved the newly sprouted beans while the crone sang about how she would enjoy eating Vasalisa for dinner. In a few minutes, she dropped the last newly sprouted bean into the third jar.

Baba Yaga was about to say, "I told you that I wanted the beans separated by sunrise and that if you failed, …"

In just that moment, the sun rose. The crone paused. The beans were perfectly separated. Her smile vanished, and she looked furious. Then she said, "Well, it's a lucky day for you, Vasalisa! You are cleverer than I expected. Put the unsprouted beans into my soup and put the sprouted beans into my salad."

Vasalisa suddenly realized that the crone had actually helped her. Baba Yaga had shouted and awakened her before the sun rose. Her wild dancing and talking had given Vasalisa time to move the last few beans. Lastly, Baba Yaga told Vasalisa to put the unsprouted beans into the hot soup. Cooking the beans would prevent any more of them from sprouting.

Vasalisa wanted to thank her, but the doll jumped in her pocket. "Say nothing. Just do as you are told," whispered the doll.

The crone watched carefully as Vasalisa looked up and said nothing. She did not call on her servant hands to do anything.

"Clever girl. Later today I will give you your fire," said Baba Yaga. "Now prepare my dinner." The crone hopped into her bucket and flew off.

5 The Fiery Skull

asalisa worked all day. She chased out the mice, took out the spiders, and shooed out the birds. She swept the cobwebs, washed the table, and scrubbed the floor.

"Do you have something to say?"

Finally, Vasalisa made dinner for Baba Yaga. She carried the water, cooked the stew, and set the table.

As the sun set, Vasalisa felt her doll jumping in her pocket.

"You are happy and full of energy," said the doll. "But be careful. Do not speak unless you are spoken to. Baba Yaga warned you not to ask too many questions. Keep your thoughts and questions to yourself. If we are lucky, we will go home today."

Vasalisa nodded. She had noticed how the crone seemed ready to pounce on her whenever she was about to say something.

Just then there was a thump outside as Baba Yaga landed in her bucket. Baba Yaga kicked open the front door. She looked around the room. Vasalisa looked down and said nothing.

"Do you have something say?" asked the crone.

"Here is your fire."

Vasalisa shook her head.

"Hmm," said the crone, sounding disappointed. "Then bring me my dinner," she commanded.

After dinner, the crone burped and went to her bed. She said nothing about giving fire to Vasalisa.

Vasalisa wanted to remind her about her promise, but she said nothing. She busied herself picking up the kitchen.

Then Vasalisa heard a gurgling sound from Baba Yaga's stomach. Mice and other critters in the room stirred nervously. In her pocket, the doll jumped and whispered quietly, "Do not say anything! Do not laugh! Plug your nose. Hold your breath. And go outside quickly. Baba Yaga is a sly one!"

Vasalisa she took a crust of bread that Baba Yaga had given her and hurried to the door. As she opened the door, she felt mice, spiders and crows brushing her legs as they fled for fresh air. She found a spot in the yard away from the fumes from the room, gave some bread to her doll, and sat down. Only then did she allow herself to smile.

When the moon rose, Baba Yaga came outside. She picked up a skull on a stick. Its eyes glowed orange and yellow. "Here is your fire," she said, handing the skull to Vasalisa.

Vasalisa bowed. She accepted the skull but said nothing.

"Carry the light wisely," said Baba Yaga. "It has great power. Mind how you use it. When its power is completely yours, the empty skull vessel will return to me."

"Lose those pigtails. You are no longer a child."

Baba Yaga jumped into her bucket and rose into the air. Suddenly, she turned back. "And one more thing," she added. "Lose those pigtails. They look silly. You are no longer a child." With that, Baba Yaga rose up into the sky.

Vasalisa felt her hair change. Her pigtails untied and her hair laid gracefully on her head.

Vasalisa turned and walked into the forest. The glowing eyes of the skull lighted the path. She found her way to her home in Noble Village without difficulty.

.

6 Vasalisa Changes the Rules

he stepsisters awoke suddenly from their sleep. Light streamed into the castle windows from the street outside. They were frightened and ran to their mother. The stepmother opened the castle door as Vasalisa approached, carrying the glowing skull.

"It is the ghost of Cinderella's father!"

"Who are you and what do you want?" she demanded.
The stepsisters saw the skull and cried out, "The ghost of Cinderella's

father has returned. He is here to avenge what we have done!"

Vasalisa felt the power and light of the skull in her hand. Then the doll jumped up and down in her pocket. "Be careful how you use the power, Vasalisa," whispered the doll. "Observe your stepfamily."

Vasalisa looked at her stepsisters. She knew in that moment that they had expected Baba Yaga to kill her. She gazed on them. Her stepsisters cowered and her stepmother trembled by the door. Vasalisa could see that her stepmother was as terrified as her stepsisters. They had become increasingly bitter and twisted as they faced loss and sorrow in their lives. Behind their cruelty, they were sad and weak. Vasalisa felt sorry for them.

She sighed. "It's me, Vasalisa. I still have my original name that my mother gave me. Most people know me by the name Cinderella. They will know me by that name in the future. So, I will answer to it." She felt the truth of her statement as she spoke.

"I brought back fire."

"As you requested, I brought back fire," she continued, looking at her stepmother. Sparks flew from the eyes of the skull, lighting logs in the fireplace and candles around the house.

Cinderella stepped into the castle. Her stepsisters and stepmother stepped back quickly. "I inherited this castle from my father," she said to them all. "You live here as my guests, not as my masters. My father wanted us to live together happily. He knew nothing of your cruelty to me. To honor his wishes, I will help with the cooking and cleaning, but you must do your parts too."

Her stepmother stiffened, and was about to say something, but Cinderella continued. "There will be further changes. Baba Yaga showed me a lost part of myself," she said. "While I was with her, I realized that I am curious and that that is good. I naturally seek knowledge. I must prepare myself for whatever life will bring."

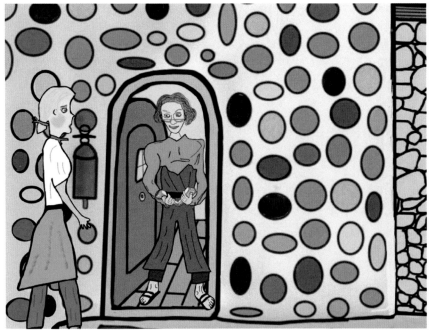

"I will request the Scholar's help in resuming my studies."

Smiling, she turned to her stepsisters and asked, "If a dog and a half eats a bone and a half every hour and a half for a day and a half, how many bones would a dog eat in a day?"

"What?" asked the first stepsister.

"There's no such thing as a dog and a half," complained the second stepsister.

"Whatever are you talking about?" demanded her stepmother.

"It's a riddle," explained Cinderella. "I like riddles. And I like to learn things."

As she stood there, Cinderella imagined herself visiting the Scholar at his Tower. She continued, "Tomorrow I will visit the Scholar. I will request his help in resuming my studies at Oberland School."

7 The Reading Club

onths went by. As she had done every week since her time with Baba Yaga, Cinderella carried a basket of cookies to the Reading Club. In the arc of her life, it would be two more years before she would go to the Grand Masked Ball.

The Scholar offered Cinderella another book to read.

Today she was with her friend, Gretel. Walking along wall around the Noble Village, they met the Scholar. The Scholar had taken an interest in Cinderella's education. When he saw them, he offered Cinderella another book to read.

When Cinderella and Gretel arrived at the study room by the Scholar's tower, the other Reading Club members were already there. This week they included Goldilocks, Bonnie Bear, Baby Bear, Jorgan, Red Riding Hood, and Hansel. Dacy, the turquoise-haired dragon girl, was also there.

Each week the Reading Club discussed what interested them. They shared their discoveries with each other. They read books on different topics, following their individual curiosities. Jorgan was reading a book by his grandfather about the forming of the alliance between Oberland Kingdom and the Dragon Kingdom of Amerland. Red Riding Hood was reading about the history of baking. She was researching the history of her grandmother, Sage, who made cookies for the Christmas Fair. Goldilocks was reading a book on business development and real estate.

Departing from the reading topics, Cinderella announced, "I want to share a riddle with everyone. I told it to my stepfamily, but they had no interest in it."

"Tell us!" begged Goldilocks, smiling.

"Since you are so interested," replied Cinderella smiling back. Everyone laughed.

"How many bones would a dog and a half ...!"

Cinderwan recited her riddle. "If a dog and a half ate a bone and a half every hour and a half for a day and a half, how many bones would a dog eat in a day?"

"Oh, my," exclaimed Red. "Word problems are not my forte."

"Nor my piano," said Goldilocks, who enjoyed word play and musical jokes.

"It is clever," admired Jorgan. "I like the distractor." Although Jorgan was a peasant boy working for the Squire, he was very smart and curious. He obviously admired Cinderella.

"The what?" asked Baby Bear, who was the youngest member of the Reading Club.

Bonnie explained.

Bonnie smiled. Turning kindly to Baby Bear, she explained. "A distractor is information that is offered but which has no use in solving the problem. In this 'riddle,' it does not matter how long the dogs ate. The dogs could munch on bones for a week or a year. That would not change the speed that they eat bones. So, saying that 'they ate bones for a day and a half' is a distractor. It distracts your focus and hinders you in finding the answer. We can ignore it."

"Wow," said Baby Bear. He liked Bonnie a lot. She was smart. But especially he liked that she was kind to him.

"What about the 'dog and a half' part. How can there be a dog and a half?" asked Red.

"My stepsister complained about that part too," grinned Cinderella.

Bonnie laughed. "That's how you know that the riddle is for fun. It's like a riddle in a folktale. In a riddle, you accept some nonsense. Mathematically, you just treat 'dog and a half' as a 'quantity of dog.' Of course, that is silly, but it is fun."

Jorgan added. "There is a math gift, too. The dog and a half quantity cancels the bone and a half quantity. This makes the math easier. When you cancel them out, you are left with a riddle that simply says, "A dog ate a bone in an hour and a half."

Everyone was quiet. Then Baby Bear brightened, "So a dog eats two thirds of a bone each hour, or sixteen bones per day."

Cinderella smiled. "You got it, bear cub!"

Everyone clapped. "It's not a proper riddle, though," observed Red Riding Hood. "It lacks an unexpected interpretation of an obscure fact."

"It also lacks the confusing trick of using words with double meanings," added Goldilocks.

Bonnie nodded, "With riddles you have to keep your wits about you. You need to discern what is important and what is not."

8 Continuing Studies

*Y*ears later, when Cinderwan was about to train in the Space and Time Element, she sat again in the Scholar's study room meeting with Baba Yaga.

"We have completed nearly a year of formal training."

Baba Yaga had the appearance of a young woman. She wore the robes of a scholar.

"I see the light in you, Cinderwan. Master of Four Elements, and student of mine."

"I see the light in you, Baba Yaga. Master of the Space and Time Element, and my revered teacher."

Baba Yaga smiled, "The time threads drew me to help you when you were a child. I came in a form that was appropriate for your age and development."

Baba Yaga continued with a smile, "My 'Witch in the Woods' had quite the costume, don't you think?"

Cinderwan smiled back. Baba Yaga had frightened her when she was a child. She said, "I am honored, Master Yaga. You have taken a hand in guiding my life since I was a child."

"Coyote was there when Marie Gottmothercus arrived."

"If not *pairs* of floating hands," laughed Baba Yaga, recalling her disguises and scenes in the hut. "You will do no less as a Master of Space and Time. Reflect back. What was the purpose of your childhood lessons in the dark forest?"

Cinderwan's teacher had opened today's training with drill and practice. Cinderwan thought about it. "There were multiple purposes. Obedience, patience, and discernment were part of it. However, the main purpose was to show me how to create space so that my life could evolve. I had to give up old ways of being. I needed to make space for the next chapter of my life's purpose."

"Yes!" said Baba Yaga. "You needed to grow yourself for your next purpose in life. You were to become a princess and a queen."

Baba Yaga continued, "Now again, you need to develop your vision. Your coming identity will be as a Five Element Master. You need to master the Space and Time Element. A Space/Time Master sees some of what is ahead. A Space/Time Master needs to make preparations now for what is to come."

Cinderwan observed, "You always knew when I *almost* asked a question, broke the silence, or disobeyed your instructions."

She continued, "I have been puzzling about your riddle in my mirror. You said 'There will be two babies. Which one will I save?' I know that I am expecting. Was the other 'baby" a new universe?"

Baba Yaga nodded and smiled.

"Ahh. My riddle is perhaps overloaded with meanings. What do you see about babies when you look ahead?"

Cinderwan focused for a moment and then exclaimed, "I will have twins!"

Baba Yaga smiled. "Your foresight is already sharpening. Raising twins is always full of challenges."

"May I ask another question, Master?" continued Cinderwan.

Again, Baba Yaga nodded.

"Your powers of discernment are growing stronger, Cinderwan. Elder Coyote was present when Marie GottMothercus first arrived on Earth. Many possible futures diverged from that moment. Our destiny would depend on a few small events."

Baba Yaga answered Cinderwan's unasked question, "Elder Coyote is not as meddlesome by nature as his reputation suggests. Still, he changed your mitochondrial DNA to be Zorconian. He saw that you would need to use Zorconian magic to activate the Glass Slippers."

Cinderwan smiled, "What a strange story! There are so many possible futures. How would he notice *that* possibility among so many?" she asked.

"You reached back in time and told him what to do."

Baba Yaga replied, "It was easier for him than you realize. According to him, some threads were very distinct and vibrated loudly."

She continued, "You reached back in time and told him what to do."

Cinderwan heard the truth of this.

"Do you remember the doll in your pocket?" asked Baba Yaga.

Cinderwan had not realized that Baba Yaga knew about the doll. She nodded.

"Does it remind you of anyone?" she asked sweetly.

Cinderwan reflected that the doll looked like a grown woman in a monk's costume. She had not thought of that doll for years. The doll was the image of Cinderwan the Elder.

"Someone had to reach back through time to animate that doll," observed Baba Yaga casually.

Then began the last part of Cinderwan's training in the Space and Time Element. She was learning the workings of causality in the Multiverse.

9 Two Androids and a Coyote

*U*num, Charley, and Emma walked along the forest trail. They were leaving the encampment in the Hidden Valley. They were heading to the Noble Village.

"Do you notice anything unusual?"

"If you two are not too busy," inquired Unum, "I would like to show you something."

Charley was curious about the visiting Zorconians. "I have time," he said. He turned to Emma and asked, "Emma, when are you expected back at the Fairy Godmother's cottage?"

Emma thought about her chores. "I can spare an hour or two," she replied.

"What I want to show you is just above the Elf Village on a mountain ledge," said Unum. "Let's pick up our pace a bit so that we can get there quickly."

The three of them raced up the mountain. They ran much faster than people can.

When they got there, Unum asked, "Do you see anything unusual?"

Emma answered first. "Three landing crafts are hidden in the ground here," she replied.

Charley added. "Energy weapons were discharged here. Also, a fourth landing craft is buried deeper. It arrived several years before yours."

Unum nodded. "That is Marie's landing craft."

"None of the landing craft are operational now," added Emma, "because Zorcon power is very limited."

"Exactly," said Unum. "The crisis on Zorcon is why I wanted to talk with you," he added. "As you may surmise, we are currently stranded here. But the energy problems on Zorcon are much graver than you may think."

Emma connected to the Zorcon University Library. She frowned. "Oh, my. Zorcon is facing grave dangers," she confirmed.

"Do you think that the Sol #3 people could help us?" asked Unum.

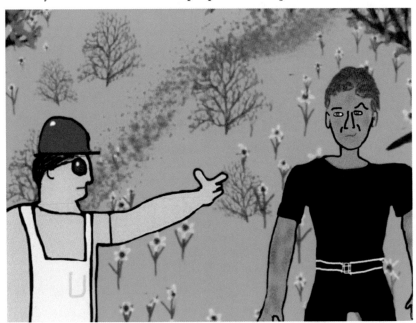

"Tell me about the magic users."

Emma blinked. "Most of them are quite primitive," she answered, "but a few have anomalous abilities."

"Duo thinks that there are travelers from other worlds among them," added Unum. "They seem to command *very* advanced technology."

Charley thought about the "magic" he had witnessed from Papa Bear, Sage, and Cinderella.

"Tell me about the magic users," commanded the Oversight agent to Charley.

Charley felt Unum's compulsion command. At the same time, he realized that his obedience circuits were disabled. He was free to ignore even a direct command.

Charley smiled at Unum. Charley thought about the command. The 'magic users' were his friends. He scanned Unum. Unum had an interior titanium skeleton and a partially cybernetic brain. This was not what he expected.

"I sense much titanium in you," he said to Unum. To any Zorconian, this observation implied that despite his outward appearances, Unum was not human. Charley had suggested that Unum might be an android, and that Charley did not need to obey him.

Unum was startled. His titanium skeleton was covered by layers of living tissue to conceal his construction.

In the woods nearby, a coyote howled.

As Charley spoke, several things happened. Emma's scanners were blocked. Her eyes stopped glowing and the operation of her internal systems was suspended. A coyote howled in the woods nearby.

10 Alliance

Suddenly, a yellow bubble formed around Unum, Emma, and Charley. Outside the bubble, time stopped. Zorcon communication was cut off.

"Nice entrance, Mr. Coyote."

The coyote appeared as they took the situation in. Elder Coyote was in his human form, except that he wore his coyote head.

"Nice entrance, Mr. Coyote," quipped Charley, who had been spending time with Hansel and was starting to sound like him.

Coyote smiled. He waited quietly for a few moments to allow everyone to realize that they were in no immediate danger. Then he switched to his completely human form.

"I am sorry to arrive unannounced," he said. "Emma understates Zorcon's emergency. Unless something is done, Zorcon will be engulfed by its sun in a few days. I am here to suggest that we work together in the mutual interests of Zorcon and Earth."

Coyote turned to Charley. "How are you doing?"

Charley smiled. "I am fine, thank you. But something is wrong with Emma. Did you freeze her?"

Coyote shook his head and then turned to Unum. "You have been observing the Zorcon situation for many years indeed," he continued.

"Yes," replied Unum. "I have been searching for a solution to Zorcon's energy crisis. My titanium body has been disguised. It is supposed to be secret."

"Much depends on keeping my titanium body secret."

Unum continued, "I am sorry that I suspended Emma. I shut down Emma's systems as a precaution, to prevent her from reporting Charley's speculations about my titanium body to any unclassified Zorcon systems."

Coyote smiled, "Your history is rather more complex than Charley realizes," he said. "We can keep your secrets safe."

Without explaining more, Coyote turned to the suspended Emma. His eyes glowed bright yellow. Coyote's glance rocked Emma like a blast of static electricity. She leaned into the intensity as her skin rippled in hot and cold waves. Her stomach twisted and then settled. She opened her eyes. Emma woke up. She caught her breath. She looked the same, but she was changed.

"We will need Emma to help us," commented Coyote casually.

"What just happened?" Emma asked.

She started to babble as her systems restarted. "Unum gave Charley a compulsion command, but it didn't work. Then Charley implied that Unum is largely titanium. Oh, my, it's true! Unum is largely titanium. He looks human, like I do. Is he an android?"

Emma paused for a moment and said, "I just pinged him. He does not respond with an android identifier."

Emma continued, "Now we are inside a time bubble. This situation is an anomaly."

Then Coyote waved his hand and Emma calmed. Coyote smiled kindly at Emma and said, "You will be OK."

Emma became quiet. She watched everyone and listened.

Coyote turned to Unum. "You asked about 'magic users.' That description is more accurate than calling us interstellar visitors. My ancestors are from Earth, but my lineage is somewhat complicated. I am here to invite you to help us to address Zorcon's situation."

"Will you compel us to cooperate?" asked Unum.

"Not at all," replied Elder Coyote. "But if you refuse, angels will weep."

"What are angels?"

"What are angels?" asked Emma.

"That's complicated," answered Elder Coyote. "I believe that you will learn about them soon. I will share some information with you now. Keep it to yourselves. To begin, my colleagues and fellow 'magic users' are Earth's Elders. I am called Elder Coyote."

Still mimicking his friend, Hansel, Charley said, "Wow. Elders are cool."

"Androids typically provide information when they are asked," cautioned Unum, thinking about the information that Coyote was conveying and surprising himself.

"With your permission, I can help with that," suggested Elder Coyote. Emma felt a tingle as Coyote made further adjustments in her.

"Oh my," shuddered Emma. "I am changed again. Somehow, I feel that I have just been given a big responsibility."

Coyote nodded. "You are right, Emma," he said, "With freedom comes responsibility."

Elder Coyote continued, "The main events ahead depend on Queen Cinderella. She is balancing her responsibilities. She will ask for your help."

The conversation inside the time bubble continued for several hours. It was the beginning of an alliance.

11 Council on Zorcon

remier Bobrowicus paced in the Council Room. He was meeting with members of Zorcon's High Council. Zorcon's current crisis was as challenging as any that a Premier had faced.

"In a few days, our sun will turn red and engulf Zorcon."

"My dear councilmen, our sun is expanding and turning red. In a few days, it will engulf Zorcon. Our 'excessive needs' are doing us in."

There was murmuring around the Council.

"Surely the engineers have a solution!"

"Tell them to do something."

Dufusicus, the Vice-Premier, spoke next. "The engineers must find a solution quickly!"

The Premier waved them to be silent. "Bear with me," he continued.

"The engineers must find a solution quickly!"

"For centuries, this Council has sought to improve the lives of our citizens. Every year Zorconians live longer. Diseases have been conquered. Poverty has been banished. Over the last few centuries, citizen entitlements have increased to include exotic foods, entertainment, and levels of consumption that were once considered lavish."

There were more rumblings. Dufusicus spoke, "Yes – and this has brought about the greatest 'Golden Age' in Zorcon's history!"

The Premier cautioned, "These 'improvements' have also required enormous amounts of energy. A century ago, our engineers suggested tapping into our sun's core to make more energy available. Our scientists warned that there were risks and that this approach was not sustainable. Other people said that the scientists were too conservative."

There was nodding and some chuckles around the room. Premier Bobrowicus continued, "This Council approved their plan to tap the sun's core. For many years our living standards have improved, and our energy demands increased."

"Now must everyone cut back?" asked one of the councilmen.

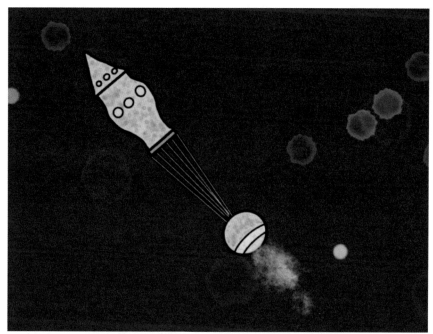

"We have a few transport ships ready."

The Council Room was quiet. They already knew the answer, and Premier Bobrowicus voiced it. "Unfortunately, it is already too late. The changes to our sun are not reversible. We cannot save Zorcon. Still, there is a way to save a few people and to give our civilization another chance. We have a few transport ships ready for settlers on Sol #3."

The council erupted with questions.

"Who would be saved?"

"What about the others?"

The Premier raised his hand. "Indeed, these are matters to be discussed. I must oversee the selection of settlers and warriors. We adjourn now for an hour. Then we can discuss this matter."

12 Initiation

he Phoenix, Baba Yaga, and Cinderwan stood outside the pyramid on the North Pole. Charley, Emma, Unum and Elder Coyote watched them. The Phoenix squawked.

"I must confer with the Phoenix."

Cinderwan nodded, but she was lost in thought. Baba Yaga had finished training her in the Space and Time Element. Mama Bear had mentioned that the Phoenix had been around "since the beginning." Now Cinderwan understood. The Phoenix was there at the beginning of the universe. He was there at the beginning of its time. She began to understand more her future role as a Master of Five Elements.

Looking at Elder Coyote, she requested, "Please ask Jorgan to join me when he can."

Cinderwan turned to her friends and said, "I must confer with the Phoenix."

The Phoenix bowed. The pyramid door opened, and they stepped inside. The door whispered shut behind them. The Phoenix spoke, "I see the light in you, Elder Cinderwan, novitiate Master of Five Elements."

Cinderwan shivered. Her proper response at this moment was a variation of the familiar Elder greeting. Cinderwan bowed and said, "I see the *early* light in you, Master Phoenix, Master of the Five Elements."

Cinderwan saw the Phoenix's novitiate ritual.

"The Phoenix nodded. "The Five Element ritual continues the cycle of creation. It has been repeated countless times."

Looking back along the time threads for the Phoenix, Cinderwan saw a young Phoenix in an earlier universe. He was undergoing his own novitiate ritual.

The Phoenix continued, "Now you see the role of a Five Element Master. I was here at the beginning of this universe. I watched the Ancients awaken. The Ancients influence everything. They orchestrate events. After you have received the transmission for the Five Elements, you will become a midwife for this universe and the birth of the next one."

Cinderwan nodded. There had been hints about her role during her training.

"Shall we discuss this, Master Phoenix?"

The Phoenix clicked, "That would be logical."

Cinderwan continued, "An unbalanced sun is not the usual course of creating universes, right?"

The Phoenix squawked. Cinderwan already knew the answer. "I never heard from my masters of this happening before, but their collective vision is limited to a few thousand universes."

"You never returned to your home universe."

Cinderwan examined the time threads surrounding the Phoenix. His threads began with the creation of the universe. She observed, "You have never returned to your home universe, have you?"

The Phoenix nodded. "I asked my teacher about this possibility. She told me that new Masters of Five Elements sometimes ask about returning home. She said that it has never been done. Finding a way 'home' is elusive."

"I am expecting," added Cinderwan, bluntly. "I want to raise my children with my husband, in Oberland Kingdom. Creating a new universe would take me away for billions of years."

"The problem has always been finding the *direction* of home."

The Phoenix clicked. Referring to the birth of universe, he said, "The midwife role is demanding." Even though his speaking was in squawks and clicks, Cinderwan sensed that he cared. "However," he added, "*Time* is not the obstacle. Time runs separately in each universe."

Cinderwan swallowed. The Phoenix was right. Time in one universe did not synchronize with time in others. Time was not the problem. Perhaps a way home could be found.

"The problem in the Multiverse," continued the Phoenix, "has always been *finding the direction* of home. You can't simply follow back along the strings from your home universe. You will use a Black Hole in this universe to create a Big Bang for the child universe. As you go through the Black Hole, the strings that connect you to your home universe are melted in the Big Bang."

"To perpetuate, universes must have children."

Cinderwan was awed by the wonder of it all. She pondered, "Universes do not last forever. Eventually all of the stars will stop shining and cool down. For life to perpetuate, new universes *must* be created. Universes must have 'children'!"

"That is the universe's cycle of creation," intoned the Phoenix.

He continued, "When a new universe is 'born', it goes through several stages in waking up. It begins as a very hot and dense point. It develops and expands. Gravity appears. New forces arise. The tiniest building blocks appear – plasmas, quarks, hadrons, leptons, photons. After many years, matter and the elements form. At the right time in the new universe, the Elements awaken. They manifest as the Ancients of the new universe."

He saw tears in Cinderwan's eyes. How could she bear to raise her children in a new universe?

Cinderwan looked ahead in the time threads. Her children's future was not the only issue. Others were at risk. She said, "The Zorconians will all perish when their sun expands."

The Phoenix nodded. He also looked through the time threads. "Unless" he said, leaving the thought hanging.

"Unless I take the Zorcon planet with me when I go through the Black Hole," continued Cinderwan, understanding the possibility. She would not be alone in the new universe. She and her children would be accompanied by a planet full of Zorconians.

"The Zorconians will perish when their sun expands."

Elder Coyote's meddling had made Cinderwan and her children genetically Zorconian. A future life on Zorcon was possible, but she was not happy about it.

"The Zorconian civilization is out of balance. Their excessive use of energy created their crisis. They would bring their habitual lack of balance with them to the new universe."

"Yes," acknowledged the Phoenix. "If you take the Zorconians with you, you must also contend with them."

Cinderwan nodded.

The Phoenix bowed and its eyes turned ember. Cinderwan felt a tingle as the lineage of Five Element Masters acknowledged and accepted her. She accepted her duty and her role.

13 A Parting

inderwan's initiation was now finished. The pyramid door opened, and the Phoenix stepped out to the North Pole plain. He bowed to everyone there, turned, and flew into the sky.

King Jorgan and Queen Cinderella came together.

Cinderwan stepped through the doorway. King Jorgan approached her. They smiled at each other. They came together and hugged.

"Let us speak privately," suggested Queen Cinderella.

The King and Queen stepped into the pyramid. The door whispered shut behind them.

Jorgan looked at his wife, lovingly. "You are expecting," he said, "but it is not yet showing. Soon you must leave on your journey."

Cinderwan turned to him. She had tears in her eyes. "The Phoenix has never heard of a case where a Five Element Master returned home. But it must be possible! I will try to find a way."

"I brought you something from Mama Bear."

Jorgan thought for a moment and said, "The Zorconians have powerful and unique resources. Papa Bear told me that they have thinking machines that can search through the possibilities, much faster than we can. Perhaps using the thinking machines, a way home can be found."

Cinderwan brightened. "I had not thought of that," she said. "I wonder whether other Five Element Masters had access to thinking machines. I will ask the androids for their help."

"I brought you something from Mama Bear," said Jorgan. He uncovered the picnic basket to reveal a berry pie.

"Eating for three?" Cinderwan asked shyly.

Jorgan and Cinderella hugged.

Jorgan smiled, "Mama Bear picked the berries in the Hidden Valley."
The royal couple talked for hours.
Finally, they held each other and hugged.

14 Emma's Loophole

utside the pyramid in what seemed like only a few minutes, the pyramid door slid open. Jorgan walked over to Elder Coyote. Coyote opened a portal and they departed for Oberland Kingdom.

"I hope that you can help me."

Cinderwan turned to Unum, Charley, and Emma. "Please come in," she said. "I hope that you can help me."

Emma, Charley and Unum walked into the pyramid with her and the door whispered shut behind them.

"I am working on a plan to save Zorcon, and also to return home," she said. "I need your help. I think that I have a way to save Zorcon, but I also want to find a way back home. My plan involves accelerating the decay processes in Zorcon's sun. This will create a Black Hole and then a Big Bang. We will take Zorcon with us into the Black Hole and arrive in a new universe."

The others smiled and nodded. This was an amazing idea. These concepts had been talked about in cosmology but doing this was far beyond Zorconian capabilities.

"Often the hero needs to take an indirect journey home."

Cinderwan posed her question: "How can I return here to raise my family? Can I travel back and forth between the new universe that we create and this one, our home universe?"

Unum spoke first. "I will search for a solution using quantum cosmological models." Using his Oversight privileges, Unum made a priority command to the Zorcon computer network. He connected to Zorcon University Library. He found the cosmology models and equations that had been developed by Zorconian scientists. He directed the computers to search for a solution.

Charley said, "I will search other fields of study for ideas."

Emma blinked. "This is a bigger question than I have ever considered. It is a big responsibility, and I am honored by your trust in us." She sat down on a bench and became thoughtful.

In a few minutes, Unum reported the findings of the computers. "Scientists and computers have speculated about the existence of a Multiverse. There are theories, but there has never been a way to test them. Unfortunately, the dominant models suggest that the Phoenix is correct.

Creating a Black Hole melts all of the strings that connect back to the originating universe. We will be unable to follow strings home." He sighed. "I will work to extend the theory."

Charley spoke next. "In folktales, there are stories of heroes who must take difficult journeys to faraway places. Sometimes, the hero cannot come home directly. To return home he must take an indirect journey. I am not sure how heroic journeys in folktales apply to travel between universes."

"The pie is made with berries from Hidden Valley!"

Emma looked thoughtful. She asked, "Technically, isn't the Hidden Valley a tiny and *separate* universe?"

Unum and Charley startled to alertness. Unum exclaimed, "Oh, my. You have greatly exceeded my expectations for an android kitchen maid. Our scientists never considered such a possibility!"

Cinderwan brightened, "Emma, that *is* brilliant! The Hidden Valley may provide just the loophole that we need. The Hidden Valley gives me hope!"

Charley expanded a plan suggested by Emma's observation. "So, first we need to find a string to the Hidden Valley. After we follow a string there, we can walk through the Troll's cave and return to Oberland Kingdom!"

"We will need something from the Hidden Valley to provide a 'string' leading to the Hidden Valley," observed Unum.

Cinderwan smiled again. "Mama Bear gave Jorgan this pie for me. It is made with berries from the Hidden Valley!"

"How did she know you would need that pie?" asked Emma.

"Maybe she didn't know," smiled Cinderwan slyly, "or maybe she had help. The universe works in mysterious ways."

She continued. "We have much to do. Our work awaits us."

.

15 Meeting with the Zorcon Council

hunder and lightning erupted at Zorcon's North Pole. A circular portal crackled into existence above the plain just outside Polar City. Inside, it showed Cinderwan's Meditation Pyramid near Earth's North Pole.

The Earth delegation followed Cinderwan through the portal.

Cinderwan stepped through the portal. The Earth delegation followed her. The delegation included Unum, Charley, and Emma, the Phoenix, the Scholar, Papa Bear, Ambassador Dorix from Amerland, and Elder Coyote.

Cinderwan bowed and whispered prayers of gratitude and offerings to the Ancients. Her portal back to Earth crackled shut.

Cinderwan's eyes glowed yellow. Sparks and fire erupted from her hand and rocks rose from the plain. Like the Meditation Pyramid on Earth's

North Pole, she created another small pyramid on Zorcon and also a much larger one for meeting with a Zorcon delegation.

Three flying craft raced over the horizon and landed near the group. A Zorconian delegation had arrived.

The Zorcon delegation met the Earth delegation by the Meeting Pyramid. The delegations exchanged greetings. Dufusicus spoke first.

"We apologize that Premiere Bobrowicus cannot be here for this important meeting of our governments. He is detained handling an urgency."

Queen Cinderella spoke next. "I too must extend an apology. King Jorgan is handling matters on Earth." She continued, "Much as I would like to discuss matters with you, I must make preparations to handle the impending solar emergency. The King and I trust our capable delegation to discuss matters with you and your people."

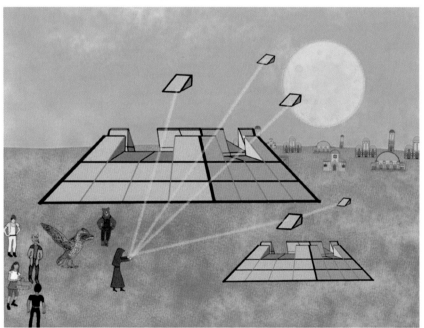

Cinderwan created a large Meeting Pyramid and a smaller Meditation Pyramid.

Dufusicus blinked. He rolled his eyes when Cinderwan said that she must prepare to handle the solar emergency. The other members of the Zorcon Council bowed but said nothing.

Cinderwan ignored Dufusicus' gestures and walked to the Meditation Pyramid. It would be her base of operations. Charley and Emma went with her. The Phoenix stayed outside to monitor the performance of his new initiate.

The delegations entered the Meeting Pyramid to discuss plans and concerns. The Zorcon High Council members sat with Papa Bear, Ambassador Dorix, and Elder Coyote. The Scientists sat with the Scholar.

"I must make preparations to handle your solar emergency."

The Vice Premier, Dufusicus, spoke first. "The people of the great empire of Zorcon welcome the Sol #3 delegation. Although this is a difficult time for us, our benevolent governance and technological leadership have served Zorcon well for many years, bringing prosperity and good living to our people. Now we face a natural catastrophe that threatens our civilization. We must make difficult choices."

The Scholar cleared his throat. He knew that Zorcon's solar catastrophe was not natural. It had been caused by the Zorconians' unsustainable energy policies when they tampered with their sun's core. Before he could say anything, Dufusicus rumbled on.

"Your Queen can busy herself in her little pyramid."

He began, "Your Queen can busy herself in her little pyramid. That does not concern us. Meanwhile, we *men* must ..."

Dufusicus paused. He belatedly noticed that the people in the delegation including Papa Bear and Professor Dorix were not all 'men.' Papa Bear cleared his throat with a low rumble.

Dufusicus looked worried, but continued, "The rest of us, however, must get down to business and deal with a serious situation. Our sun's instability limits our normal access to the energy that we need. The disaster is developing quickly. We cannot save our planet or transport all of our people."

Papa Bear nodded. Dufusicus would keep talking without leaving an opening for others to speak.

"We have made some arrangements that involve Sol #3. It is proper that we discuss our plans with you as representatives of your primitive world. Our colonization fleet will soon leave for Sol #3. When we arrive, we will inform your King which areas of Sol #3 we will take to build new Zorconian cities."

"We did not come here to divide the lands of Earth."

Coyote spoke, "My dear Vice Premier. We did not come here to divide the lands of Earth with you."

Dufusicus tried to interrupt, but Coyote raised a finger. Dufusicus choked. He realized that he had no voice. His eyes widened as he looked at the young man who was Coyote. Coyote was somehow preventing him from interrupting.

Coyote continued, "We came to offer Zorcon a new beginning. Without Queen Cinderella's rescue, your planet would be destroyed in a few days."

Dufusicus shook his head and cleared his throat. He said, "Our Oversight organization reported your Queen's idea of triggering a Black Hole and taking Zorcon into a new universe. Our best scientific minds have examined this idea. It cannot work. A Black Hole cannot be triggered. Even if it could, you could not safely take our planet into it. Even if you could, Zorcon would not arrive in a new universe."

"You come from a primitive civilization. Cinderwan exaggerates your capabilities. We of Zorcon have vastly more advanced science and technology. Your queen knows this. Her business in her little pyramid is no more than an imaginative ploy. It is a diversion to slow us in leaving for Sol #3. You must take us for fools."

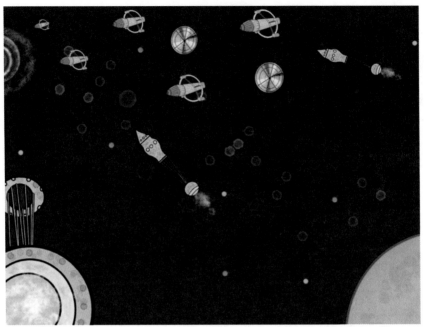

"Our fleet of warships will soon reach your pretty planet."

Dufusicus then stood and puffed out his chest. "Zorcon's civilization is far from finished," he continued. "In a few hours, our fleet of armed warships will leave for your pretty planet. The fleet will be led by Premier Bobrowicus himself."

"Your primitive tricks are no match for our wartime fleet. Premier Bobrowicus will soon arrive on Earth. He will tell your King Jorgan what to do. He will decide which lands King Jorgan can rule and which lands will be civilized by Zorcon. So, what do you think of that?"

Ambassador Dorix raised her eyebrows and looked at the Council Members. She followed her debating habit of answering questions with questions. "Zorconian ships and its technology are impressive enough, but did you really not notice that our delegation came to Zorcon without the need of any ships?"

Dufusicus looked puzzled for a moment. Perhaps he should have paid more attention, but he said nothing.

Papa Bear chuckled. The deep rumble of his voice shook the room and stopped all conversation. "Gentlemen, we acknowledge that you must keep a brave face about your planet's imminent destruction. But please refrain from threats and subterfuge. Our purpose today is not to 'save our Earth' by delaying your invasion fleet."

"We know all about your Premier's fleet. It actually departed two hours ago. We saw it enter the connecting wormhole. Later, we will decide what to do with it."

The room became quiet as Dufusicus' lie was exposed.

At just that moment, the light shining in from outside the pyramid dimmed to the darkness of night. Zorcon had not seen a dark sky for several months. Then everyone felt a series of gravitational waves before gravity stabilized again to Zorcon's normal gravity.

"Gentlemen, stop this subterfuge and nonsense."

There was an inhale of shock around the room as the Zorconians realized what was happening. Dufusicus had said it was impossible, but Queen Cinderella was doing exactly what Oversight had said she planned to do.

Elder Coyote explained, "Queen Cinderella has now placed a shield around Zorcon. That shield has darkened the sky. Your departing ships will be permitted to leave, but otherwise nothing will be permitted to go through the shield."

Coyote then winked. "We will be back on Earth long before you are. You had best leave now, if you would avoid being burned by your expanding sun."

The Councilmen looked at each other. They had vastly underestimated the Sol #3 delegation. To their surprise, the Sol #3 delegation did not tremble or bow to Zorcon's military threats. Instead, their Queen seemed to be casually doing things that were far beyond Zorconian capabilities, or even Zorcon understanding.

"Learning something about girl power, are we?"

Professor Dorix, the dragon Ambassador from Amerland Kingdom, snorted. She puffed out a burst of flame and smoke, smiled slyly at Dufusicus, and said, "Learning something about 'girl power' now, are we?"

Dufusicus glared at her.

Just then, the door of the Meeting Pyramid opened, and the Phoenix stepped in. He squawked for a moment, turned around, and went back outside.

Everyone followed him outside.

Elder Coyote spoke again, "Queen Cinderella is about to trigger your sun's collapse to a Black Hole. She is shielding Zorcon and will take it with her into a new universe. We will return now to our duties on Earth."

Unum bowed to the other Zorconians. He walked towards the Meditation Pyramid. Dufusicus called to him by his Oversight agent name, "Agent Smithicus, please join us in our return to Polar City and then to the Fleet."

Unum paused thoughtfully and then turned to the Zorcon leaders. Unum said, "I plan to assist in Zorcon's transition. I suggest that you make a public information broadcast to our citizens to prepare them for what is ahead. You might explain why our night sky has returned. Tell everyone that they will have a new sun in the morning, and a new beginning for their lives."

"I plan to assist in Zorcon's transition."

Papa Bear, Elder Coyote, Ambassador Dorix, and the Scholar joined the Phoenix outside the pyramids. Elder Coyote waved open a portal to Oberland Kingdom. They stepped through and the portal crackled shut behind them.

16 Blessing of the Angels

𝒞inderwan sat on the bench in the Meditation Pyramid. Unum, Charley, and Emma watched her.

Cinderwan reviewed her life's journey.

Cinderwan reviewed her life's journey. She saw the arrival of the Fairy Godmother on Earth before she was born. She saw Coyote's temporary theft of the Fairy Godmother's wand and his discovery of the molecular difference between human and Zorconian mitochondrial DNA. She strengthened the threads reaching back in time, bring awareness to Coyote in the past of the present she was living.

She saw herself as an infant. Elder Coyote watched over her. One day he changed her mitochondrial DNA to match Zorconian DNA. She saw her early years with her parents and the passing of her mother. Later, her stepmother sent her into the forest to meet Baba Yaga. Cinderwan relived her experiences in the forest, this time though the eyes of the doll. Still later, she saw herself dancing with Prince Jorgan at the Grand Masked Ball.

Cinderwan blinked. Her companions were watching her carefully. She smiled at them and said, "I have been thinking about my life's unlikely journey to this moment. The energy of this moment is intense as the new universe is about to born." She paused. "My memories, thoughts, concerns, and joys are vibrating back in time. They have now reached Elder Coyote on a day long ago when he was walking on the mountain above Elf Village. Elder Coyote could see this very day as a possible future. He adjusted little things. His little changes shaped the courses of our lives."

"My thoughts going back in time started Coyote's 'meddling'."

"I placed a shield around Zorcon. Time here stopped except inside this pyramid. The planet is shielded from the chaos outside."

"So, this is how the Metaverse works," thought Unum out loud, "Our actions today shape the course of possible futures. By reaching back from the future, you have guided Coyote's choices and the course of history. Such backwards causality is not possible according to Zorconian science."

"It is unintuitive," commented Charley.

"It is elegant and beautiful," observed Emma.

Cinderwan smiled at her. She recalled a poem from her Elder training.

> Vision is mind.
> Mind is empty.
> Emptiness is clear light.
> Clear light is union.
> Union is great bliss.

In that moment Zorcon's sun began to collapse. A Black Hole eerily hollowed out a place in space. Shielded and frozen, Zorcon dropped into the Black Hole. The Black Hole shuddered and collapsed to a point, sending a ripple of gravity waves across the universe.

In that instant, a new universe was born and the strings connecting Zorcon to its home universe melted. Zorcon entered the vicinity of the new universe but was not exactly in it. With a few temporal hiccups, time started in the universe.

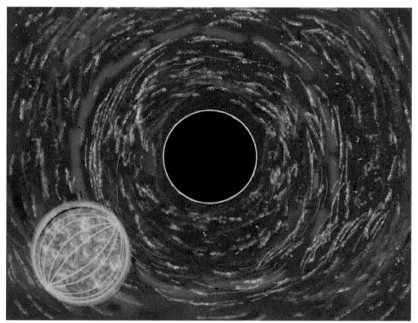

Shielded and frozen, Zorcon was drawn into the Black Hole.

Cinderwan regulated time inside the Meditation Pyramid, speeding it up and slowing it down as needed. She monitored key events as the new universe began to develop. Inside the pyramid scant seconds passed.

The seconds and ages ticked by. "The plasma period has finished," she announced. A few moments later she said, "the first quarks are appearing." From inside the protective shield, everyone was protected from the tumultuous events of the early universe. As their minutes passed, Cinderwan called out the universe's developmental phases as hadrons, leptons, and then photons appeared. Again, she adjusted the passage of time in the Meditation Pyramid.

"A "Dark Age" begins," observed Cinderwan as protons and electrons came together and made hydrogen atoms that absorbed much of the light. Hundreds of millions of years were passing in the new universe – but only a couple of minutes passed for Cinderwan and the androids. More stars formed and the hydrogen was ionized again. "And now the fog lifts," she continued, "Galaxies and other structures are now forming." There was a slight shudder as Cinderwan made some spatial and temporal adjustments. The pyramid and Zorcon entered the new universe.

Winged angels appeared in the Meditation Pyramid.

Outside Zorcon, stars were shining. Inside the pyramid, Winged Angels suddenly appeared. There was a moment of deep and penetrating silence.

The Angels spoke, "Our Five Element Master has arrived."

"She brought an entire planet with her! And some interesting friends." "The Elements awaken."

"Welcome, Cinderwan. Blessings on you, my accomplished daughter."

Cinderwan gazed up. The Angel was Bodi, her mother.

Bodi smiled. "I expected nothing less of you, my dear. You have changed the rules again."

Cinderwan rose and hugged her mother. "Mother," she asked, "how can you be here?"

Bodi answered, "My darling, the answer to your question has always been in my name, Bodi. I am a Bodhisattva *and* an Angel. As a Bodhisattva, my purpose is to assist in rising of the consciousness of all beings. I took life on Earth to be your mother, and to prepare you for your life journey."

Cinderwan could feel Bodi's love, and she hugged her tightly.

"What interesting friends you have brought with you."

"I have always watched over you," added Bodi. "We Angels orchestrate the development of universes. During the birth of each universe, we bless and awaken the Elements. We are charged with guiding and protecting the well-being of the multiverse."

Cinderwan nodded. She was worried about the Zorconians. Their desires grew so much over the centuries that they damaged their own sun. If they continued in this way in the new universe, they would leave a trail of destruction.

Cinderwan spoke, "I felt compassion and wanted to save the Zorconians. Sadly, they lack balance. They see the universe as existing only to serve their purposes. They do not recognize their responsibility to take care of it."

Bodi nodded. "The Zorconians would be a very challenging group from which to recruit and train Elders. Do you and your titanium friends have plans?"

Without waiting for an answer, Bodi turned to the other Angels who were following this conversation with interest. The Angels stood close together. Their wings faded in and out. They conferred among themselves and seemed to be focusing on the new universe outside the pyramid.

"Training a new order of beings is a very delicate matter."

In that moment Cinderwan and her companions felt a tingle. Subtle changes were occurring many layers deep in their nature, far deeper than Elder training. A vibration rippled across the fabric of the new universe. The Elements stirred. After a few moments, the Angels turned to Cinderwan.

Bodi smiled at Cinderwan. "You and your friends have our blessing."

Behind her, Unum, Charley, and Emma looked at each other and to the Angels. Cinderwan found herself remembering her Earth Element training. The woman monk on the face of the mountain had given her a cryptic message, "Training a new order of beings is a very delicate matter."

Bodi heard her thoughts. "It always is, my dear." she said. "You will face some interesting challenges."

Cinderwan smiled. "I plan to enlist help in the Elder training. When we travel back to my home universe, I will ask my own trainers for help."

The Angels bowed. Bodi spoke, "That's new. In many ways, this new universe is an experiment for you and for us. You may feel our presence in the future as we watch over you."

"We return now to the Metaverse," they said.

"Vision is mind," smiled Bodi.

The Angels disappeared.

Cinderwan and the androids looked to each other across the Meditation Room. Cinderwan felt alone and not alone at the same time.

17 Homecoming

*W*e approach a moment of truth," observed Unum. "Can we find strings back to the Hidden Valley?"

"I found the strings that will lead us back."

Cinderwan smiled. She held the pie from Mama Bear. "Dear Unum, I have already found strings to lead us home."

Cinderwan had been quietly holding the pie. Charley smirked. "And I thought you were planning to eat that pie!"

Even Emma smiled. Charley sounded more like Hansel, and she was understanding his boyish humor a little more.

"Indeed," smiled Cinderwan. "We can eat this pie soon enough. But first we should park this planet in a suitable solar system. Do any of you have suggestions?"

Unum suggested activating parts of the Zorconian computer network to search using the astronomical instrumentation of Zorcon. Time on the rest of Zorcon was still frozen, but Cinderwan made some adjustments that allowed the computer network to restart. Unum, Charley and Emma searched through star systems in a nearby galaxy.

"I have found a suitable system," announced Unum. "It has a yellow sun and few asteroids."

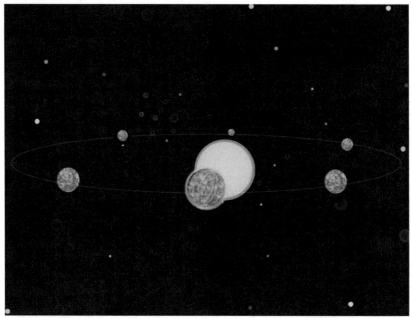

"Zorcon's new sister planets cycled through their seasons."

"Zorcon is so crowded because Zorconians always want more things," commented Emma. "Could we encourage them to rediscover Nature? Perhaps we could create something that would lead them to appreciate nature and to live with more integrity."

Cinderwan smiled and concentrated. The Angels had tuned the new universe to her. In the new universe, her power was immense. She moved Zorcon to an orbit around the yellow sun that Unum had found. She made some adjustments. Five new planets appeared spaced along Zorcon's orbit. They were new twin sisters to Zorcon but without any marks of civilization. Cinderwan seeded them with plant and animal life from Zorcon and Earth. A few minutes passed in the pyramid as eons whizzed by outside. The planets orbited their new sun like a slowly spinning necklace. Weather and storms came and went. The new sister planets cycled through their seasons.

Cinderwan felt her belly. Her children were growing. "It's time to see Papa," she smiled, patting her belly.

Cinderwan waved her hand and the door to the Meditation Pyramid slid open. Cinderwan and her companions stepped out to a dark plain on Zorcon. Except for a small area around the Meditation Pyramid, Zorcon was still in stasis and dark inside the shield.

Holding the pie, Cinderwan stretched out her hand. She found the connecting strings to the Hidden Valley. Creating a portal between universes was a tricky operation, but it was easy to find the Hidden Valley using strings from the pie.

"My Darling!"

Cinderwan opened a portal.

"My Darling!" It was King Jorgan. He was waiting for them in the Hidden Valley. He stood just beyond the portal. At his side were Mama Bear and Papa Bear. The Royal Coach was waiting, watched by Coyote. Cinderwan heard a squawk. Flying down from a nearby waterfalls, the Phoenix descended, checking on his former novitiate.

The King and Queen hugged, in a most unseemly way. "First this," whispered Jorgan as he kissed her. Then aloud, he said, "Our people are assembling to meet you in the Quadrangle."

BC, Bonnie, Hansel, and Gretel led the procession.

Cinderwan was exhausted. The ride back to Oberland Kingdom was a blur. Coyote hastily opened a portal to a spot outside the Troll's Meeting Cave. The coach took them to the bridge below the Fairy Godmother's cottage. There, BC, Bonnie Bear, Hansel, and Gretel joined them. They marched ahead, leading the procession towards Oberland School.

As they approached Oberland School, they heard sounds of a crowd.

Someone shouted, "It's Queen Cinderella!"

Preparations had been made for a big welcoming. As she scanned the many people who had come, Cinderwan thought of her many adventures with them over the previous few years.

Many villagers came to welcome Cinderwan.

She wept tears of joy. Her children would be raised on Earth. Tradition would hold. They would grow up with many friends including dragons in Amerland.

18 The Fifth Law

igh on the mountain ridge above the Elf village the songs of two flutes intertwined. At first the song of one flute would call out. Then the other flute answered in harmony. It sounded like four flutes playing as the sounds echoed off the mountain. The flutes sang of the past and of the future. The songs of the Air Masters sang the winds of change, telling of change and empowering it.

Two flutes told of winds of change.

"I see the light in you, Elder Mama Bear, Master of the Fire Element," said Baba Yaga as she bowed to Mama Bear.

"I see the light in you, Elder Yaga, Master of the Space and Time

Element."

When so many Elders gathered together, it took several minutes for all of the pairs of Elders to give their mutual greetings.

Eventually all the greeting and bowing was over and Elder Coyote started the formal part of the meeting.

"I welcome Cinderwan, our Five Element Master. Cinderwan, what can you tell us about what has happened? Zorconian colony ships and warships are heading our way. What should we do?"

"Zorconian warships are coming our way."

Cinderwan bowed. "It is a joy to be back home, here with my wise friends and teachers!"

"I wish to ask for your help. Zorcon has advanced technology. In their view, they have improved the lives of their people, but their societies use unsustainable amounts of energy. They have unbalanced the natural order."

"Elder Coyote and Elder Yaga have asked what we should do about the incoming Zorconian fleet. How would Zorconian presence influence our people, especially our children? This is an important question. After my novitiate ritual, I realized that we do not always understand what is going on."

Cinderwan smiled. "The Ancients are our partners. In my training, I did not think to ask what the universe wanted. I did not understand the role of a Five Element Master."

Papa Bear, Mama Bear, Sage, Thistle, Eagle, and Baba Yaga smiled at their young Elder colleague.

She continued, "For many years, the Zorconians lived out their individual lives. The Zorcon government made its choices. Zorcon University sent observers here. We were also busy in our lives.

After the arrival of the Zorconians some years ago, Elder Coyote altered my DNA to open possibilities for us all. His foresight was sharp. You selected me for training to become a Five Element Master. Who would imagine that behind all the scenes of our lives, a much larger story was playing out? Our universe wanted to have a baby!"

She bowed to the Phoenix and continued, "Zorcon is now asleep in a new universe. I must return to awaken them when the time is right."

The Elders met high on a mountain ridge.

The Elders had been conferring with the Phoenix, so the baby backstory about the universe was not a complete surprise. Cinderwan's account filled in a larger context.

"Also, I met with my mother, Bodiwan."

The Phoenix clucked in a whisper to Cinderwan, "I am curious. Did the Angels look like humans, perhaps with wings?"

Cinderwan paused. She had not foreseen this question. She thought back to when Emma was staring at Bodiwan. Realization dawned. This was a Five Element Question.

"In the midst of my midwifery, I met with my mother, Bodiwan."

"Yes," she smiled. Following her instincts, she looked back at the Phoenix. Quietly, she thought, "And for you, my mentor, did the Angels appear as phoenixes when you created this universe?"

The Phoenix heard her thoughts and clucked. Cinderwan waited, but she already knew his answer. The Phoenix nodded. The Angels appeared as phoenixes to the Phoenix and appeared as winged humans to her. Bodiwan was her mother, but she was also an Angel. She could take on the form of any Five Element Master. This was how Angels greeted new Five Element Masters during each time of universe creation.

Cinderwan blinked. This was a lot to take in. Turning to the Elders, Cinderwan said, "Bodi is a Bodhisattva and an Angel. She has overseen the creation of many universes within the Metaverse."

Papa Bear smiled. This was really a big picture, but he had suspected something like this.

Cinderwan continued, "She gave her blessing. New universes are always being created. The Angels watch over them and awaken the Elements. A Five Element Master must create a school for Elders and work with the

Ancients. The Angels are watching over our newborn universe as an 'interesting experiment.'"

She continued, "The Ancients are manifestations of the Elements. In the new universe, the Ancients are stirring. I must return to establish an order of Elders there."

Earth's Elders raised their eyebrows.

Cinderwan nodded. "Usually, a Five Element Master waits for life to begin in the new universe. She seeks out that life, selects Elder candidates and trains them. Things are happening a little out of order in this new universe. The Zorconians are already there. They sleep in a time bubble. Some of their relatives are in a fleet in orbit above us now. They do not all understand that their world and families are asleep and will be happy to see them in the new universe."

"So, life already exists in the newborn universe, but the Zorconians have a strong cultural bias. It would be at odds with the caretaking responsibilities of Elders."

Coyote nodded and said, "It would be quite a challenge to find suitable candidates for Elders among the Zorconians."

"I propose training androids to be Elders."

"Yes," said Cinderwan. "The Zorconians have been blind to their responsibilities as caretakers. I plan to change the traditional approach of selecting and training Elders. I ask for your help. The new universe with Zorconians is a big challenge, and I have a family to raise!"

Mama Bear smiled. She thought about her challenges in parenting BC.

Cinderwan continued. "Some of you have gotten to know the androids, Charley and Emma. I am also impressed with Unum. He is not exactly an android like Charley and Emma, but his nature has similarities. In designing androids, the early Zorconian robotic scientists encoded strong behavioral guidance deep in their minds." She then stated the First Law of Robotics.

> "A robot may not harm a human, or, by inaction, allow a human to come to harm."

She continued, "Coyote has already changed Emma and Charley to be free of their Zorconian obedience. For his part, Unum is very long lived and has accepted a responsibility to watch over humanity."

The Elders were listening.

"Rather than training Zorconians, I propose training Unum, Charley, Emma and other future *liberated androids* to become the Elders of the new universe."

The others inhaled in surprise.

Cinderwan continued, "I ask for your help in training them."

Around the room and in the minds of the Elders, this idea vibrated.

"That is a most intriguing idea."

Cinderwan continued. "Also, reflecting on the role of Elders, there is an additional 'law' to recognize."

> "An Elder may not harm the sentient Metaverse, or, by inaction, allow the Metaverse to come to harm."

The Phoenix squawked. The Elders understood him. It meant, "Now that is the most intriguing idea that I have heard in a long time."

About the Author

Mark Stefik and his wife, Barbara Stefik, live in northern California. Mark is a computer scientist and inventor. Barbara is a transpersonal psychologist and researcher. They illustrate the stories together.

They can be contacted through their website at

www.PortolaPublishing.com

Made in the USA
Middletown, DE
30 April 2021